PAUL BUNYAN AND BABE the BLUE OX

→ THE **GREAT PANCAKE ADVENTURE** ←
BY **MATT LUCKHURST**

ABRAMS BOOKS FOR YOUNG READERS
NEW YORK

This is the story of a man and his ox.
The man's name was

He was taller
than the trees and larger
than life, and he forever changed
the American landscape.

People remember him and
his best friend

as the greatest lumberjacks
to ever work in the forests.
What folks usually do not
remember is how that came to be.

Paul was a very big boy, born in a very small

town on the banks of the St. Lawrence River.

At school, Paul had to squish
his way into the classroom.

He was not a

He was far more interested in
studying his favorite thing to eat:

"Math," Paul said,
"is just not very tasty."

The countryside grew every kind of

VEGETABLE AND FRUIT

but Paul and Babe wanted pancakes.

Paul's mom sat them down for a talk.
"You have to start eating the food we

GROW

You are going to get sick if
all you eat is pancakes!"

She gave them each some broccoli,
but when Paul and Babe tried it they

SPAT

it right out.

"These green things are for the rabbits.
What big guys like us need are pancakes!" said Paul.

So Paul's mom cooked pancakes all day
and night, and her son and Babe greedily gobbled
up each and every delicious one.

Being a growing boy and ox,

THEY COULD EAT A LOT!

"I just cannot keep feeding
you and Babe all these pancakes,"
Mom said, panting. "I have fields to tend."

Paul and Babe tried to help Mom
by working in the vegetable fields,
but their big feet just

everything in sight.

Paul's and Babe's appetites had become too big
(and so had they).

One day they decided it was time
to follow their stomachs and find their

PANCAKE
FORTUNE

out in the great big world. So Paul hugged
his mom and promised to write, and he
and Babe took off into . . .

Soon, Paul's and Babe's heads were in the clouds
and their stomachs were rumbling like

So much so, they barely heard the man
who was calling to them.

"We've got a big problem down on
the Syrup River!" he yelled. "I need a couple
guys with big appetites to come help out."

Paul bent down and looked him straight in the eye.

DO YOU HAVE PANCAKES?!

The man laughed.
"We've got more pancakes than even you can eat,
or my name ain't Brimstone Bill!" he said.
"We will see about that!" Paul replied.

When they got to the river, it was a

A truck had rolled over and dumped its load
of flour into the river, whipping up a sizable
amount of batter, which had caused a log jam.

The hot summer sun soon had that batter sizzling up
into more pancakes than Paul and Babe had ever seen! Their
dream had come true! They put on their best

and went to it!
They ate and ate and ate pancakes until . . .

Paul's shirt buttons

When every last pancake had been eaten, the logs swept down the river without a problem.

Bill could not believe  his eyes

"Why don't you and Babe come work for me, logging the land? I'll pay you as many pancakes as you can eat!"

Paul and Babe enthusiastically agreed.

Up and down the country Paul and Babe
tromped and stomped with Bill.
From Wisconsin to California,
up the Little Garlic River
and down
the Onion,

THROUGH

TALL-WOLF
COUNTRY

and across the Beartooth Plateau,
Paul and Babe helped log the land.

Out west, Paul and Babe tried to level the ground by filling valleys with pancake batter.

When the sun came up, the ground grew hot and started to cook. Up popped a whole

MOUNTAIN RANGE RIGHT in FRONT OF THEM!

The mountains used to be bigger, but Paul and Babe were hungry and snacked on some of them.

Because of their uneven appearance, folks called them the

Down along the Colorado River,
a stray pancake got picked up by a

and Babe took after it.

Paul tried to hold him back.
He dug his heels into the ground.

When Babe finally caught the pancake,
he and Paul had dug up a huge swath
of dirt that is now called the

But one day Babe's bright blue glow
began to fade. He was feeling sick.

He just lay there like

Paul was worried—and not feeling so good himself. Bill called a doctor to come and examine them both.

The doctor said, "You seem to have been

EATING TOO MANY PANCAKES!

Paul exclaimed.

"That's impossible! There is no such thing as too many pancakes!"

The doctor explained to Paul and Babe that they needed to balance their diet and eat different foods or they would both become even more ill.

Paul figured they had better do
what the doctor said.
But where could they find enough

GOOD FOOD

for them both?

Paul thought for a moment.
Where? Where? Where? Then it hit him!

Paul and Babe said their good-byes to Bill.

When they got back home,
Paul's mom was mighty glad to see them.

And sure enough, there was
plenty of healthy food for them
both. Soon Babe turned bright
blue again.

"See? Your mom is always right!"
Paul's mom said proudly.

From that day forward,
they stayed in town, growing

BUNYAN
SIZED
Veggies

and helping the townspeople
and always listening to
what Mom said—and of
course eating a heap
of fruit and vegetables!

And that is how Paul Bunyan
and his best friend Babe changed
the American landscape and became the

GREATEST
LUMBERJACKS
EVER

And they never ate any
fluffy, delicious pancakes ever again . . .

Well, every now and then
they might sneak

(Just don't tell Mom.)

Author's Note

I grew up on Vancouver Island, British Columbia, Canada. My grandfather was an immigrant from England who worked as a logger for many years, eventually owning his own sawmill, called Raven, on the Campbell River. My dad also worked at the mill. Thanks to the presence of the forest, the river, and the mill, and thanks also to Mom's Sunday morning pancakes, I was drawn to stories about Paul Bunyan from a very young age. Today my grandfather's mill and the land around it are a nature reserve and public park.

Some historians trace Paul and Babe back to the mid-1800s in the northern woods of Wisconsin and Michigan. Others cite sources saying that the character hails originally from Canada, especially Quebec. Whatever the original source, stories of Paul Bunyan's prowess eventually stretched clear across America and Canada, traveling from camp to camp by word of mouth among the loggers who worked the forests. It was the Red River Company of Minnesota that made Paul Bunyan a household name back in 1914, with its advertising campaign for lumber that featured the larger-than-life lumberjack.

In researching this book, I spent weeks digging through the stacks of the New York Public Library. I pored over as many stories of Paul and Babe I could get my hands on. Then I used a mix of collected tales and historical documents to compile a story that, while unique in structure and theme, stayed true to the oral tales of Bunyan and Babe. It is well documented that Paul and Babe loved pancakes, as do I, and this became the driving narrative for the story. It is also true—just less well known—that produce grown on Bunyan's "home farm" provided giant veggies to feed his men. (In many of the Bunyan stories, Paul himself has a camp of loggers; in my story, I decided to keep the focus on Paul and Babe, but I kept in the giant fruits and vegetables.)

I took particular inspiration from a small mention in *Transactions of the Wisconsin Academy of Sciences, Arts and Letters*, which says of a Bunyan story: "The teller of the tale . . . has two motives: first he wishes to excite wonder; second, he wishes to amuse." And certainly as lumber camps moved west and the lore of Bunyan grew, so did the tales, becoming more and more spectacular, as the men of the north woods wove increasingly intricate stories exalting his great feats. It is in the tradition of exaggeration and hyperbole that I interpreted the tales of Paul and Babe.

So today when I am gobbling up pancakes in the various breakfast haunts of Brooklyn, New York, and plotting my next escape back to the great outdoors, I am reminded once again of Paul and his great blue ox—and also that I should pick up some broccoli on the way home.

TO MICK, PAM AND JOE

Select Bibliography

Edmonds, Michael. *Out of the Northwoods: The Many Lives of Paul Bunyan, with More Than 100 Logging Camp Tales*. Madison, Wis.: Wisconsin Historical Society Press, 2009.

Felton, Harold W. *Legends of Paul Bunyan*. New York: Alfred A. Knopf, 1947.

Feuerlicht, Roberta Strauss. *The Legends of Paul Bunyan*. New York: Crowell-Collier Press, 1966.

Hoffman, Daniel. *Paul Bunyan, Last of the Frontier Demigods*. East Lansing: Michigan State University Press, 1952.

Laughead, W. B. *The Marvelous Exploits of Paul Bunyan: As Told in the Camps of the White Pine Lumbermen for Generations During Which Time the Loggers Have Pioneered the Way Through the North Woods from Maine to California*. Minneapolis, Minn.: Red River Lumber Co., 1929.

McCormick, Dell. *Paul Bunyan Swings His Axe*. New York: Scholastic Book Services, 1963.

Robins, John Daniel. *Logging with Paul Bunyan*. Ed. Edith Fowke. Toronto: Ryerson Press, 1957.

Shephard, Esther, and Rockwell Kent. *Paul Bunyan: Twenty-One Tales of the Legendary Logger*. Orlando, Fla.: Harcourt, 1952.

Stevens, James. *Paul Bunyan*. New York: Alfred A Knopf, 1925, 1947.

Stewart, K. Bernice, and Homer A. Watt. "Legends of Paul Bunyan, Lumberjack." *Transactions of the Wisconsin Academy of Sciences, Arts and Letters*, vol. 18, part 2 (1916), pages 639–51.

Turney, Ida Virginia. *Paul Bunyan Marches On*. Portland, Ore.: Binfords & Mort, 1942.

Untermeyer, Louis. *The Wonderful Adventures of Paul Bunyan*. New York: Heritage Press, 1945.

The illustrations in this book were made with gouache on paper. The font is Luckhurst Hand Drawn.

Cataloging-in-Publication Data has been applied for and may be obtained from the Library of Congress.
ISBN: 978-1-4197-0420-8

Text and illustrations copyright © 2012 Matt Luckhurst

Book design by Matt Luckhurst and Chad W. Beckerman

Printed and bound in China
10 9 8 7 6 5 4 3 2

Abrams Books for Young Readers are available at special discounts when purchased in quantity for premiums and promotions as well as fundraising or educational use. Special editions can also be created to specification. For details, contact specialsales@abramsbooks.com or the address below.

THE ART OF BOOKS SINCE 1949
115 West 18th Street
New York, NY 10011
www.abramsbooks.com